The Mystery of
the Lost and Found Hound

The Mystery of the Lost and Found Hound

By Lynn Hall

Illustrated by Alan Daniel

GARRARD PUBLISHING COMPANY CHAMPAIGN, ILLINOIS

Library of Congress Cataloging in Publication Data

Hall, Lynn.
   The mystery of the lost and found hound.

   (A Garrard mystery book)
   SUMMARY: A girl and her brother's efforts at
tracing the owner of a lost beagle leads them to
involvement with dog thieves.
   [1. Dogs—Fiction. 2. Mystery and detective
stories] I. Daniel, Alan, 1939-   II. Title.
PZ7.H1458Myl   [E]   78-27502
ISBN 0-8116-6408-2

CONTENTS

1. Sandy Discovers a Mystery 7

2. The Secret Numbers 16

3. Sandy Looks for Answers 27

4. A Dangerous Mission 39

5. Police to the Rescue 51

CHAPTER 1

Sandy Discovers a Mystery

"Ninety-nine, one hundred. Here I come, ready or not."

Sandy heard her brother's voice, but she had forgotten about their game. Behind the rocks where she'd planned to hide, Sandy had found a dog.

The dog was a small hound, black and brown and white. She was just sitting there, for she was tied to a tree by a heavy chain. At the sight of Sandy, the little dog wiggled and whined.

"Who did this to you?" Sandy asked. She was angry.

"You are supposed to be hiding," Ted called, as he climbed the rocks toward Sandy and the dog.

Ted and Sandy always played hide-and-seek on the afternoons when their family came to the park. While the children played, their parents fished in the trout stream. Sometimes Sandy got bored with the game and wandered off to explore by herself. She was in love with the rambling mountain park, the jagged rocks, and the dark pine forests. She liked to explore them alone. She had planned to do that today, after a short game of hide-and-seek.

Now something new held her attention. Here was the little dog.

"Go get mom and dad," Sandy said to Ted. He turned and ran to get them.

Mr. and Mrs. Cassals came up the steep path.

"Somebody left this dog here," Sandy said. "Look. They chained her up and left her behind to starve to death." There was anger in Sandy's voice.

Mrs. Cassals leaned over and patted the dog's head. "Poor little thing." She turned to her husband. "Can you get this chain unfastened?" she asked him.

"Maybe we'd better leave her," Mr. Cassals said. "Her owner may be around here somewhere."

But the rest of the family did not agree. "Tell you what," Mr. Cassals said. "I'll go and get a park ranger." He went off toward the ranger station.

Sandy sat down beside the dog and held her. "Don't worry, little puppy. I'll take good care of you."

Sandy stayed with the dog while the ranger and her father looked for the dog's owner. No one knew anything about the little hound who was tied to a tree. Then the ranger called the camping area office. None of the campers had signed in with a dog like this one. No one had reported a missing dog.

"We could take her home," Sandy said for the eighth time. "We could keep her until we find her owner."

Finally her parents agreed to take the little dog home. "We can't leave her here to starve," Mr. Cassals said.

"But we can't keep her," Mrs. Cassals told Sandy, as they got into their car. "One dog is enough. Silly is going to be jealous as it is."

Sandy and Ted laughed at that. Their small gray poodle had been known to drive away dogs twice his size. He did not want his family to pet other dogs.

As they drove away, Mr. Cassals asked Sandy, "Do you know anyone who raises beagles around here? You know all the dog owners. Someone might know who owns this dog."

Sandy thought for a minute. She knew people who raised German shepherds and Saint Bernards. She knew of a kennel where Afghan hounds were raised, and a place where coonhounds were kept chained. There was a boarding kennel she loved to visit. But she did not know anyone who raised beagles, like this little lost hound.

They drove narrow roads toward home, through lovely blue-green mountains on the northern edge of the Ozarks. Red boulders dotted the slopes, and scrub pines hung onto the ground by ropelike roots. Cattle grazed in the valleys, while foxes and deer kept them company.

Sandy loved the view along these roads, but she had seen it so many times she didn't think about it today. All she could think about was the little beagle curled up on the seat beside her. Someone must own her. Who? And why would he be so cruel? Why would he leave the little dog alone and frightened in the woods? Who could have done that?

Suddenly she had an idea. "How about those new people?" Sandy asked her father. "The ones who live on Cox Creek Road in that old house. They've got lots of dogs, maybe a hundred, all kinds of them. Maybe this dog is one of theirs."

"It wouldn't hurt to stop and ask," her father said. "It's not far out of our way."

After several miles they turned onto a

narrow, rocky road. This led to a smaller track over a shaky bridge, and then ended. To the left was a barn that sagged against the tall hillside. Sandy could see daylight through the barn's wooden sides. To the right was a run-down house. Cardboard covered many of the windows.

No one seemed to be home. But at the sound of the car, dogs began barking inside the house. It did indeed sound like a hundred dogs.

Sandy looked down at the beagle beside her. The little dog shook as she leaned against Sandy.

Suddenly a woman appeared in the doorway. She was tall and worn, and there was no sign of welcome on her face. She stayed behind the screen door.

"Go ask her, Sandy," her father said.

Slowly, Sandy got out of the car and

carried the little dog toward the house. With every step the little beagle seemed to become even more frightened.

Sandy opened her mouth, but before she could speak, the woman said, "Where'd you get that dog?" It was hard to see into the dark room, but it seemed to Sandy that the woman grew pale as she looked at the beagle.

"We found this dog in the park. Is—" Sandy began.

The woman stopped looking at the dog and met Sandy's eyes. There was anger in her look, and fear.

"She isn't my dog. Get out of here with her. This is private property."

The woman slammed the door.

Sandy turned and walked back to the car. Deep fear touched her. Something was wrong. Sandy knew it.

CHAPTER 2

The Secret Numbers

It wasn't until they reached home that Sandy remembered what the woman had said. The family was in the kitchen watching the little beagle eat a dish of Silly's dog food. The poodle lay under a chair and whined under his breath about the strange dog in his house.

"That old woman said 'she,'" Sandy thought. "'*She* isn't my dog.' And I was carrying the hound under my arm. The woman couldn't tell if it was a boy or girl.

How did she know the dog was a female if she'd never seen her before?"

Aloud Sandy said, "The woman in that house where we stopped knew this was a female dog before I said anything. And did you see the way the woman looked at the dog? It was almost as if she were afraid of this little hound."

Mr. Cassals said, "A lot of people are afraid of strange dogs, you know."

"Yes, but daddy, there was a whole houseful of dogs in there. You heard them barking. And besides, the little beagle was just as frightened as the woman. Look." Sandy pointed to the dog, who was eating the food and wagging her tail at top speed. "She's not the least bit afraid of us. But she was frightened when we were at that house."

The dog finished eating and came over

to Sandy. She wagged her tail and then lay down to have her stomach rubbed. Silly, who was crouched under the chair, growled and whined.

Ted had not been very interested until now. Suddenly he said, "What's that writing on her leg?"

They all looked. In neat blue figures half an inch high, on the dog's inner leg, were nine numbers.

"It looks like a tattoo," Mrs. Cassals said. She ran her finger over the numbers.

"It is," Sandy cried. "There is such a thing as tattooing a dog. I saw a booklet about it the last time we were at the vet's. Let's call him and ask. There's probably some way we can find her owner from the tattoo. He'll know how."

"We're not going to bother him at home on a Sunday evening," Mr. Cassals said

firmly. "Tomorrow morning is soon enough. You can call him then," Mr. Cassals told Sandy.

That was fine with Sandy. She spent the evening paying special attention to the little hound. First she gave the dog a bath. The clean coat was a lovely black, orange, and white. Then she dried the beagle with a big towel. Next, she put the dog on her lap. Silly tried to climb up, too.

When Sandy went up to bed, the beagle went with her. The little dog curled up beside Sandy. Silly, who usually slept with Ted, also jumped up on Sandy's bed. He lay down as close as he could to Sandy. He stared hatefully at the other dog.

Early the next morning, Sandy called Doctor Patrick's office. Mrs. Patrick, who helped in the office, answered. Sandy told her about the dog and the tattoo.

"Oh, yes," Mrs. Pat said. "That means the dog is listed with the National Dog Registry in Carmel, New York." She gave Sandy the phone number. "Just call and tell them about the dog, and give them the tattoo number. They'll have the owner's name on file."

Sandy thanked her and hung up. Just then her father came through the room from his office. His office was a glassed-in side porch off the living room. He sold insurance there. He was carrying his empty coffee cup and heading for the kitchen.

"What's all this about?" he asked. "Did you find out about the tattoo?"

Sandy waved the paper with the registry's phone number. "Mrs. Patrick says to call this place and they'll tell us who owns the dog. May we call? Now?"

He looked at the number. "That's in

New York. The call will cost a lot of money, but I guess we should do it. Some people must be very worried about their pet." He looked at the beagle, who was curled up in the softest chair in the living room. Silly was no longer growling at her, but he stayed close by and watched her.

Mr. Cassals went back to his office to make the call. Sandy followed, excited to be on the trail of the dog's owner. When Mr. Cassals got the number, he talked to someone on the other end.

"Who is her owner?" Sandy asked as he hung up. She tried hard not to jump up and down.

"They won't give me the owner's name," he told her. "The woman I talked to at the registry said that some people do not like to have their names given out. So instead, she took our name and phone number. She said she would call the dog's owner, and the owner will probably call us."

Sandy sat on her father's big desk and stared at the phone. It didn't ring. Mr. Cassals got up and went into the kitchen for a second cup of coffee. Suddenly the phone rang. Sandy grabbed it.

A woman's breathless voice said, "Hello, hello. Do you have a beagle there? Is she

all right?" In the background Sandy could hear children's voices shouting, "Gwennie-Beagle! They've found Gwennie-Beagle!"

"Yes," Sandy said. "We found her here in the park yesterday. She's fine. She's sleeping on a chair in the living room."

"Oh, thank goodness." The woman's voice sounded a little teary. "We thought we'd never see her again. What park did you find her in? Where do you live?"

"In Big Spring Park," Sandy answered. "We live in town, 503 Frederick Street."

"But what town?"

"Van Buren," Sandy said, puzzled at the question.

There was a pause. Then the woman asked, "Van Buren, New Mexico?"

Sandy was even more puzzled. "No. Van Buren, Missouri."

"How did Gwennie get all the way from

New Mexico to Missouri?" the woman asked. But she did not wait for an answer. "You are hundreds of miles from us," she told Sandy. "We live in Clayton, New Mexico. I took Gwennie to the shopping center Friday morning, and somebody stole her from the car. I'd locked it, for I'm always careful about locking it. Listen, is your mother or father there?"

Sandy handed the phone to her father and listened while plans were made and directions given. Gwennie's owners would drive to Missouri the next weekend to pick up their dog. Sandy hardly heard what her father said, for her mind was busy with a new puzzle. Or was it a new piece of yesterday's puzzle?

Last Friday morning someone had stolen Gwennie from a parked car in New Mexico, hundreds of miles away. Then, just two days later, Gwennie was found chained to a tree in a state park in Missouri. How had the hound traveled so far? Who, or what, had taken her and then abandoned her? And why?

The woman in the farmhouse had known Gwennie and had pretended *not* to know her. Why? And what had made the woman afraid of the dog?

That woman knew the answers. Sandy was sure of it. And now, right now, Sandy was going to find some of the answers.

CHAPTER 3

Sandy Looks for Answers

Sandy was mad. She came out of the police station and kicked hard at her bike's kickstand. "The policemen wouldn't even listen to me," she thought angrily. "Okay then, I'll have to do something about this myself."

She rode to the edge of town, to a small white house sitting far back from the road. Behind it was a long, low building with

fenced runs along one side. A sign hung
outside, "Shady Lane Kennels—Boarding,
Grooming."

Sandy left her bike under a tree and
went toward the kennel. She had been
there often enough to know where to find
Mrs. Lane at this time of the morning.
The buzzing of electric clippers led Sandy

to the grooming room at the front of the kennel.

Mrs. Lane was small, with tan and gray hair and a freckled face. She was grooming a little schnauzer. When she saw Sandy she turned off the clippers and smiled.

"Hi, there, Sandy. How's my good little helper this morning?"

"I'm okay, but I need to ask you something." Sandy sat on a dog crate. She loved to watch Mrs. Lane groom dogs, but today her mind was too full of other things.

"Now what's on your mind?" Mrs. Lane asked, as she began to comb the dog's legs.

"Do you know anything about dog thieves?" Sandy asked.

Mrs. Lane laughed. "Why? Are you thinking of becoming one? Or are you serious?" She looked again at Sandy.

"I'm serious. We found a little beagle yesterday out at the park. She's named Gwennie. Somebody had tied her to a tree and left her there. She has a number tattooed inside her leg, so we called the National Dog Registry. They found her owner, and the owner is coming to get her, so that part of it is okay. But the owner lives in New Mexico. The woman said somebody stole the dog out of her car last Friday morning."

Sandy waited for this to sink in. When Mrs. Lane nodded and looked toward her, Sandy went on.

"There's more," she said. "On our way home from the park, we stopped at that old house out on Cox Creek Road. You know, where they have all those dogs. I thought there might be a chance that Gwennie belonged to them. When I took Gwennie up to the door, she really was frightened. She shook and held on to me. The woman who came to the door acted funny, too. She looked at Gwennie and said, '*She's* not my dog,' and I hadn't told her whether Gwennie was a boy or a girl. So how did she know? She acted almost as frightened as Gwennie did."

Mrs. Lane combed the schnauzer's beard

and eyebrows forward and trimmed them neatly with her scissors. "So what are you thinking? That the woman is a dog thief?"

Sandy put her hands in her pockets. "I don't know," she said. "Yes, I guess I was thinking something like that. It is strange about Gwennie, and they do have lots of dogs out there. They haven't lived around here for very long, and they don't seem friendly like other people."

Mrs. Lane looked thoughtful.

Sandy went on. "The thing is, I don't know anything about dog thieves, or even if there are any. But why would anyone have stolen a dog in New Mexico? And why would that person have chained the dog to a tree in Missouri? It doesn't make sense."

Mrs. Lane carried the schnauzer to the metal bathtub and began bathing him.

Sandy followed. Mrs. Lane worked the shampoo through the dog's coat. While she worked she told Sandy, "I've read a bit in dog magazines. There *are* dog thieves. In fact, I understand that stealing dogs is becoming a big business. Groups of thieves work together in different parts of the country. The dogs stolen in one part of the country are taken by truck far away where they are not known. Then, hundreds of miles away from their homes they are sold."

"Who will buy the dogs?" Sandy asked.

"Sometimes pet shops do. Or the thieves may sell dogs to laboratories where the dogs are used for experiments. Sometimes the thieves run ads in newspapers and sell dogs to families. But usually they don't steal tattooed dogs because laboratories and pet shops won't buy them. It would be too easy to prove that the dog was stolen. So if dog thieves happen to get a tattooed dog, they usually turn it loose or get rid of it some way. They don't want it traced to them, for they would be arrested."

Sandy thought about this while Mrs. Lane dried the schnauzer. Finally she said, "Then it makes sense, doesn't it? Gwennie was stolen by dog thieves and brought out here. They found her tattoo and left her in the park. So that woman out on Cox Creek Road must be one of the thieves, or else her husband is."

Mrs. Lane said, "That could very well be. I think you should stop by the police station and tell them about this. They'll probably want to look into it."

Sandy shook her head. "No. I was just there. They wouldn't listen. They treated me like a little kid." Her voice was angry.

"Then I'll give them a call," Mrs. Lane said.

"No, I'll take care of it myself." Sandy stood up and started toward the door.

"Now wait, Sandy. Don't go and get yourself into any trouble. These people are very likely thieves. If they are, they might be dangerous. They could be making a lot of money from this dog business, and if they think you know about them—"

But Sandy was already on her bike. "I won't do anything dumb," she called back.

When Sandy got out to the road again, she sat down with her foot against a weedy bank. She thought about what must have happened to Gwennie, about the sadness and fear Gwennie's family felt while she was lost. Sandy thought about all the other stolen dogs and the people they belonged to. There must be thousands of sad and

lonely people whose dogs have been taken, she thought to herself.

Sandy wondered how she would feel if Silly were stolen. She didn't let herself think what might happen if he were sold to a laboratory and had to live in a cage and be used in experiments. He'd be frightened, hurt, and maybe killed.

Her face grew hard. She pushed away from the bank and turned her bike toward Cox Creek Road. Somebody had to do something to stop those thieves. It looked as though it would have to be her.

She rode faster and tried not to think about Mrs. Lane's warning. *Dangerous.* Well, maybe. Fear and excitement were all mixed up inside her.

CHAPTER 4

A Dangerous Mission

Sandy hid her bike under the shaky little bridge, and then she hid in the head-high weeds that grew nearby. She could see the old farmhouse and the barn. How could she get to the house and barn without being seen? There were trees here and there, not too far away, and there was plenty of long

grass and horseweed. With luck, she could make it safely to the house. Once there, she could find out if anyone was at home.

She made her way carefully from one tree to another until she was behind the house and near an open window. She could hear a man's angry voice inside the house. He was talking to someone. It must be the woman I saw, Sandy thought.

By peeking through the lace of a lilac bush, Sandy could see the people inside. The man was holding a shotgun.

"Don't you lie to me," he shouted. "You didn't shoot that beagle like I told you to. This gun hasn't been fired since I left here Saturday night. It's still loaded. What did you do with that dog?"

"Oh, all right," the woman said in a tired voice. "I didn't see any reason to kill such a nice little dog. I took it to the park and left it. I thought somebody would find it and give it a home, thinking it had been left behind by campers. It was a nice little dog, Jack. I didn't want to shoot it."

"Women!" the man shouted at her. "You don't have the guts for this business. I knew that all along. The least you can do is to get me some lunch."

They moved out of Sandy's sight, into another room. Sandy slipped around the corner of the house, hoping to hear more of what they said, something that she could tell the police. But then she saw the barn. Its doors were standing open, and a large truck was inside.

"If I could get the license number of the truck," she thought, "that would be something to tell the police. It must be the truck he uses to carry the stolen dogs. The police might have some record of it.

Maybe somebody saw it being used to steal dogs and reported it." When she tried to think it through, she wasn't sure how important the truck might be. And yet all the time on television shows, police tracked criminals through car license numbers. It was worth a try, she decided.

She worked her way back to the trees and then around the house. From the last tree to the barn door there was an open space of about thirty feet. Sandy didn't really want to cross it, but she made up her mind. From that distance she could see that the truck's front license plate was covered with mud. She couldn't see the numbers.

"I'll have to run across there fast," she thought to herself. "If that man sees me, I'll be in real trouble. I can go around to the back of the truck. If I have to wipe

the mud off that license plate, at least I'll be out of sight."

She took a few deep breaths. Then she ran hard and fast, and ducked into the barn. Even though the sunlight was coming in between the old boards of the barn, it was dark enough inside to make Sandy feel

fairly safe. She moved along the wall to the back of the truck. It was like a moving van, but smaller. At the back, one of the big double doors stood partly open.

Sandy dropped to the floor and crawled toward the rear license plate. The truck was backed up almost to the barn wall.

She couldn't stand up. Instead, she turned around and sat.

The license plate was in front of her face, but it was too dark to read it. She ran her fingers over the plate, brushing off the mud. Then she felt each letter and number with her fingertips. "AR77-6102."

She felt it again and again as she said the number over and over. She wanted to be sure she remembered it. This was important. She *had* to remember this number.

As she started to crawl away, her arm caught the corner of the license plate. It made a singing noise. Suddenly, terrifying sounds started around her head. After a second Sandy realized the sounds were the barking of many dogs inside the truck. Loud, booming barks, high, shrill yips, and hound-yodels all doubled and then redoubled within the metal walls of the truck.

Sandy's heart beat so hard it made her arms and legs shake. At the house, a door slammed. She heard the sound of running toward the barn.

Fearfully, she looked from side to side. There was no place to hide. In terror Sandy climbed into the truck and pulled the door shut behind her.

"Now I'm really trapped," she thought. Sandy moved farther into the big truck, feeling her way in the dark. She felt wire mesh, a large cage of some sort that seemed to run the entire length of the truck. Her arm hit a handle.

Outside the truck, the man's voice yelled, "Is somebody out here? Is somebody on my property? Get out here where I can see you!"

Without thinking, Sandy moved the handle that opened the cage door. She slipped inside. Immediately she was covered with the warm, bumping bodies of dogs. They climbed against her, sniffing, licking. Sandy was so full of fear of the man outside that it didn't occur to her to be afraid of the dogs. She stayed down in the farthest corner of the giant cage and prayed that the dogs would hide her if the door opened.

"There's nobody here, Jack." The woman spoke from the yard.

The truck's door was tried, jiggled, but not opened. The man muttered something, but Sandy could not understand what he said. For a few minutes she heard voices but not words. Then, suddenly, the driver's door in the cab opened and slammed shut.

"Be about a week, ten days," the man called from inside the cab. "I'll deliver this load to Chicago, then work my way back through Indiana and Kentucky till I get another truckload. It might be two weeks. If there's any trouble about that hound with the tattoo, you give me a call at the Chicago number. Then I'll keep clear till it's safe to come home."

The truck started and eased out of the barn. Sandy huddled in the dark, her eyes wide with fear. She was going to Chicago!

CHAPTER 5

Police to the Rescue

After a few minutes, her mind cleared. Sandy thought, "Maybe I'm not so trapped after all."

She crawled through the dogs toward the cage door. Its latch was shut but she was able to reach through the wire and open it. She climbed through and shut the door behind her.

"Now for the hard part. Maybe." The truck bumped slowly over the rough dirt road. Sandy crawled toward the truck's door. In the dark she could see nothing. When she reached it, she ran her hands along the metal face of the double doors.

There was a handle on one of the doors.

Relief came over her as she pulled it down and felt it give. She opened the door a crack and held it there. The road slipped away behind the moving truck, too fast for her to jump.

In her mind she pictured the country road they were on. Soon they would be coming out onto the highway that led north. He would be turning there, she

thought, to go to Chicago. He would have
to stop at the highway. That would be the
place to jump out.

The truck went down a hill, then up.
Yes, they were almost there. Sandy braced
herself. The truck slowed, almost stopped,
but suddenly began to pick up speed as
it turned onto the highway.

"Now!" She shoved the door open and
jumped.

She landed, sprawled and scraped. But as soon as she got her breath, she was up and running. It was half a mile to the edge of town, then four blocks to the police station. She ran hard, her legs pounding. Blood dripped from her cut knees.

Outside the police station, a black and white police car was just pulling away from the curb. Sandy ran toward it, waving. After one look at the frantic, bleeding girl, the policeman stopped and started to get out.

"Dog thief, in a truck, is going that way," Sandy puffed as she pointed with her finger.

"Get in," the officer said. Sandy jumped into the car beside him. He turned on a switch and the siren sang.

"It's a gray truck. The license number's

AR77-6102. I know! I was in the back of the truck. He's got a lot of stolen dogs, and he's taking them to Chicago to sell. Then he was going to steal some more on his way home. I heard him tell her. His wife, I guess."

The car roared through town. Sandy

looked out the window just as they passed Ted. He was on his bike in front of the drugstore. She loved the look of surprise on her brother's face. She patted her bloody knees.

"Tell me what this is all about," the officer said. Sandy told him.

They were out of town and several miles up the highway when Sandy sat forward. "That's him, up there."

The truck pulled over at the sound of the siren. The police car swung in front and stopped.

"You stay here and stay down," the officer told her.

Sandy needed no urging, but she tried hard to hear what was happening. The

static from the police radio made it almost impossible.

In a few minutes the officer was back. He reached for the radio's mike and called for another car. Within minutes two highway patrolmen drove up. Sandy looked back at the dog truck. The man, Jack, was being handcuffed and led away. One of the patrolmen was climbing into the truck.

When the policeman came back to Sandy,

he was smiling. "Well, young lady, you certainly did your good deed for the day. You're going to be quite a heroine around here."

Sandy grinned and glowed. Her knees didn't hurt nearly so much when she thought of the fun of being a heroine. A patrolman drove the truck back to town, and Sandy and the policeman followed.

When they got to the police station, the policeman helped Sandy inside.

"What will happen now?" she asked him.

"First we'll get those legs of yours patched up and let your parents know you're okay. Then we'll need you to make a statement. Where did you say this guy lived? There was a woman out there, too?"

She told him about the house on Cox Creek Road, and he gave the information to a policeman behind the desk.

"What will happen to the dogs?" Sandy asked.

"We'll do our best to trace the owners, starting in New Mexico, where you said the beagle was stolen. Thank goodness for that tattoo—and for your quick mind. Dog stealing is a dirty thing. You can feel darned good that you helped put one operator out of business." He rumpled her hair and winked at her.

That weekend, when Gwennie-Beagle's family arrived from New Mexico, they were told the whole story. The local newspapers had come to take pictures of Sandy and Gwennie, and the story had covered most of the front page of the newspaper.

"We're just so glad to have her back," Gwennie's owner said. She hugged Gwennie

and cried a little, while the children all tried to hug their dog at the same time.

Silly pressed into the crowd for hugs, too, and everyone laughed.

Sandy tried not to think of the other dogs who had shared that brief, terrifying ride with her. Some of them might be

returned to their families. Probably most wouldn't, but at least they would find other homes. The newspaper story had brought forth dozens of offers to adopt the unclaimed dogs.

"At least they won't end up in a laboratory," Sandy thought. She looked down at her legs and admired the impressive brown lumps of her knee scabs.

All in all, it had not been a bad week.